For Caitlin, who loves both foxes and rabbits.
C.W.

Thank you especially to Mum, Dad, and Andy,
and my closest friends for being a constant source
of inspiration and support.
C.P.

OXFORD
UNIVERSITY PRESS

Great Clarendon Street, Oxford OX2 6DP

Oxford University Press is a department of the University of Oxford.
It furthers the University's objective of excellence in research, scholarship,
and education by publishing worldwide in

Oxford   New York

Auckland Bangkok Buenos Aires Cape Town Chennai Dar es Salaam Delhi Hong Kong
Istanbul Karachi Kolkata Kuala Lumpur Madrid Melbourne Mexico City Mumbai Nairobi São Paulo
Shanghai Taipei Tokyo Toronto

Oxford is a registered trade mark of Oxford University Press in the UK and in certain other countries

Text © Carrie Emma Weston 2004
Illustrations © Caroline Pedler 2004

The moral rights of the author and artist have been asserted

Database right Oxford University Press (maker)

First published 2004

British Library Cataloguing in Publication Data available

ISBN 0-19-279099-4 (hardback)   ISBN 0-19-272546-7 (paperback)

1 3 5 7 9 10 8 6 4 2

Typeset in Slimbach

Originated by Dot Gradations Ltd,UK

Printed in China by Imago

Moonlight Lily

Carrie Emma Weston

Caroline Pedler

OXFORD

UNIVERSITY PRESS

All was quiet on the farm.

The lights had gone off in the farmhouse.

The cows were in the cowshed.
The hens were in the hen house.
The sheep were in the sheep
pen with their lambs.

All the animals
   were sound asleep . . .

      . . . even Lily,
         the white rabbit.

Far away
an owl hooted
in the dark.
Out of the woods,
and into the
moonlight,
crept a fox.

He slipped through
the cornfield,
and into the farmyard.

Past the barn,

past the hen house

and past the cowshed, he trotted,

until he came to where
Lily the rabbit slept.

Then…

BOO! he said.

'Finlay!' cried Lily. And she jumped for joy.
Lily and Finlay had long been friends.

'It's Finlay,' clucked Henrietta to the other hens. 'Quick! Or we'll miss the moonlight dance!'

Lily and Finlay loved to dance. And the other animals loved to accompany them.

So Henrietta gathered the hens. Together they began to cluck softly.

There was a low *moooooooooo* as the cows joined in.

Then the sheep began too, with their lambs baa-baaing.

The old owl hooted.

The cat caterwauled.

The mice squeaked.

And the donkey clip-clopped his hooves to the rhythm.

Lily and Finlay whirled around the farmyard,
and Lily led the dance.
First, a waltz…

…followed by a tango…   …they tried a quickstep…

and then…

…a foxtrot, of course!

Lily and Finlay bowed to the musicians. Everyone clapped.

Lily was quite out of breath, but there was more to come …

… for Finlay was a master magician.

Bunches of flowers appeared
from old buckets.

Strings of knotted hankies
unravelled on…

…and on…

…and on…

…and on.

Finlay saved his best magic until last.
He reached behind Henrietta's ear and pulled out…
…a speckled egg!

That always made the hens cluck with laughter.

No one wanted the moonlight
party to end. And Lily had
one more game to play...

There!

The scarecrow had a *much*
better view from the top of the
haystack! And he was very
pleased with his new nose.

'How the farmer will scratch
his head in the morning!'
laughed Lily.

All too soon
the sky began
to get lighter.

The old owl
had gone to bed.

The mice had
scurried home.

The cows yawned.

The lambs dozed.

The cat was just about to
shut her eyes when ...

'Cock-a-doodle-doo!'

shrieked the cockerel loudly.
(He just loves doing that.)

It was time for Finlay to go. 'Don't you want to come with me?' he asked Lily. 'Then you could dance whenever you like.'

Lily looked out across the fields. The wild rabbits were still dancing in the dawn light. Then she looked back at her hutch. 'The children would miss me so much…' she sighed. 'And they might think you had been eaten by a fox!' laughed Finlay. 'Well, until another night then, Moonlight Lily!'

And with a flash of his tail, he was gone.

The sun rose and the cockerel crowed loudly.

The farmhouse door swung open. The farmer looked around the farmyard and across the field to the haystack. He scratched his head.

All *seemed* quiet on the farm.

Until, that was, the children came out to feed their rabbit!